LETTERS FROM A
DESPERATE DOG

EILEEN CHRISTELOW

Clarion Books / New York

For Emma's best friend!

Clarion Books
a Houghton Mifflin Company imprint
215 Park Avenue South, New York, NY 10003
Copyright © 2006 by Eileen Christelow

The illustrations were executed in pen and ink and watercolor.
The text was set in 18-point Elysium.

www.houghtonmifflinbooks.com

Printed in Singapore

Library of Congress Cataloging-in-Publication Data

Christelow, Eileen.
Letters from a desperate dog / by Eileen Christelow.
p. cm.
Summary: Feeling misunderstood and unappreciated by her owner,
Emma the dog asks for advice from the local canine advice columnist.
ISBN-13: 978-0-618-51003-0
ISBN-10: 0-618-51003-6
[1. Dogs—Fiction. 2. Advice columns—Fiction.] I. Title.
PZ7.C4523Let 2006
[E]—dc22   2005032744

TWP 10 9 8 7 6 5 4 3 2 1

I live with George, the painter, and his cat.

Usually we all get along fine.

But sometimes George gets on my nerves. He can be so unreasonable! For instance, take this morning.

I'm happy to be outside! I start to discuss my woes with the dog next door, but, of course, George interrupts.

I head for the newsstand, where I pick up a copy of the *Weekly Bone*.

Then I scrounge a couple of cinnamon buns at the Sidewalk Café and catch up on the news.

I race across the street to the library and e-mail *Ask Queenie.*

To: qdog@weeklybone.dog
From: emmadog@mutts.dog
Subject: George

Dear Queenie,

I'm a pup with a problem. My human, George, barks way too much. It's "Bad! Bad! Bad!" all day long. The least little thing sets him off. He's really getting on my nerves. What should I do? Please answer quickly!

Sincerely,
A desperate dog

I don't have to wait long for an answer.

So I try to make George feel better.

I would have been better off taking a nap on the couch.

Late that night, when I'm sure George is asleep, I use his computer to e-mail *Ask Queenie* for more advice.

To: qdog@weeklybone.dog
From: emmadog@mutts.dog
Subject: GEORGE!

Dear Queenie,

I am the most unappreciated dog in the world. I tried to make George feel better, but your advice didn't work at all. It's still "Bad! Bad! Bad!" all day long.

Yours truly,
An unappreciated dog

P.S. He even called me useless!

To: emmadog@mutts.dog
From: qdog@weeklybone.dog
Subject: GEORGE!

Dear Unappreciated,

USELESS!? My paw! You must show George he can't live without you. Do you help around the house? Do you keep an eye on things? Do you live up to your canine responsibilities? If so, you needn't worry.

Keep that tail wagging!

Queenie

I admit I don't keep an eye on things as much as I should. So that night I decide to be extra-vigilant.

14

Unfortunately, the cat has a point.

17

But I'm not fast enough!

I'm in real trouble now!

As soon as the library opens, I e-mail
Ask Queenie for more advice.

To: qdog@weeklybone.dog
From: emmadog@mutts.dog
Subject: You-Know-Who

Dear Queenie,

I'm the most misunderstood dog in the world. I did my best to keep an eye on things around the house. But did I get any thanks for my efforts? NO! It's just "Bad! Bad! Bad!" Not even a pat on the head! From now on, I'm going to be like the cat and just nap on the couch all day long.

Yours truly,
Misunderstood

To: emmadog@mutts.dog
From: qdog@weeklybone.dog
Re: You-Know-Who

Dear Misunderstood,

A famous sheepdog once said, "What every dog needs is a job! There are far too many dogs in this world who lie around on the couch waiting for the next free meal." I couldn't agree more! There are many interesting jobs listed in the *Weekly Bone*. A new career will get you off the couch and away from George's tirades.

Keep that tail wagging,
Queenie

19

Luckily, the library has a copy of the *Weekly Bone.* I flip to the want ads.

I hurry over to the theater. Several dogs are already waiting in line.

By the time it's my turn to audition, I'm pretty nervous.

21

But there's a problem. Within hours, I'm on a bus with my fellow actors, speeding away from home, the cat, and George.

Each night we perform in a different town.

I'm a BIG hit! But I can't stop thinking about George.

Finally, after several weeks on the road, we return to perform *On the Couch* in my hometown. I scramble off the bus. We only have a short time to get ready. Then I notice the "Missing" posters.

To: george@painters.art
From: info@travelingtroubadors.ode
Subject: Your missing dog

Dear George,

Be sure to attend tonight's performance of *On the Couch*, an award-winning drama starring a brown-and-white dog. I'm one hundred percent certain it's her!

Yours truly,
A helpful friend

That night I give my best performance ever.

As we're taking our bows, I hear a familiar voice.

We promise I'll return the next day, and then George and I head home.

We stop for gas.

27

But, then, of course, there's a problem.

For some reason, George can't open the truck door.

It's more than my tired brain can deal with. I need something to chew to calm my fraying nerves.

By the time George finally climbs back into the truck, we're both in a bad mood.

And that is exactly what we do!
But it's not quite the end of the story.

Late that night, when I'm absolutely certain George is asleep, I borrow his computer to e-mail *Ask Queenie.*

To: qdog@weeklybone.dog
From: emmadog@mutts.dog
Subject: My new career

Dear Queenie,

Thanks to your excellent advice, I am now a famous actress! But even better, George and I are friends again. He has finally realized what a wonderful dog I am.

Sincerely,
A happy dog

P.S. However, this probably won't be my last e-mail. You know how unpredictable George can be!